DREAMING
IN COLOR

DREAMING IN COLOR

Melanie Florence

orca soundings

ORCA BOOK PUBLISHERS

Published in Canada and the United States in 2020 by Orca Book Publishers.
orcabook.com

Library and Archives Canada Cataloguing in Publication
Title: Dreaming in color / Melanie Florence.
Names: Florence, Melanie, author.
Series: Orca soundings.
Description: Series statement: Orca soundings
Identifiers: Canadiana (print) 20200176056 | Canadiana (ebook) 20200176064 |
ISBN 9781459825864 (softcover) | ISBN 9781459812918 (PDF) |
ISBN 9781459812925 (EPUB)
Classification: LCC PS8611.L668 D74 2020 | DDC jc813/.6—dc23

Library of Congress Control Number: 2020930604

Summary: In this high-interest accessible novel for teen readers, a young teen
is thrilled when she gets into art school but shocked to learn that
some students feel she doesn't belong there.

Orca Book Publishers is committed to reducing the consumption
of nonrenewable resources in the making of our books. We make
every effort to use materials that support a sustainable future.

Orca Book Publishers gratefully acknowledges the support for its
publishing programs provided by the following agencies: the Government
of Canada, the Canada Council for the Arts and the Province of British
Columbia through the BC Arts Council and the Book Publishing Tax Credit.

Edited by Tanya Trafford
Design by Ella Collier
Cover photography by Gettyimages.ca/J Prichard (front) and
Shutterstock.com/Krasovski Dmitri (back)

Printed and bound in Canada.

23 22 21 20 • 1 2 3 4

For Taylor. May art school be the first of many great adventures.

Chapter One

Jen loved this time of day, when everyone was still asleep and the house was silent except for the sound of the clock ticking in the living room. The sun was coming up, painting the sky in shades of pink, purple, orange and red. The colors matched the paint she had loaded on her paintbrush. She studied the canvas propped up on the easel by the window.

She created some of her best work in the early hours of the morning when everyone else was asleep.

As the sky slowly got brighter and brighter and the birds outside got louder and louder, Jen added the finishing touches to her painting. Happy with the final result, she stretched her back with a low groan.

"How long have you been up?" her mom asked from the studio doorway. Jen's dad had converted the sunroom for her so she had somewhere to work and store all the art supplies that used to clutter every available surface.

Jen yawned. "I don't know—since five thirty maybe?"

Her mom stepped into the room. She leaned over Jen's shoulder and studied the painting. "You finished!" she said, taking a sip of her tea.

"Yeah. What do you think?"

"I think it's beautiful, honey."

"Thanks. I wanted to get it finished before my art school audition today."

Her mom looked at Jen over the rim of her teacup. "Which pieces are you choosing for your portfolio?" she asked.

Jen looked around the room and frowned at the canvases propped up against the walls and the drawings tacked to every surface.

"I'm not sure yet. A couple of paintings—and I still want to do a multimedia piece with the feathers you gave me. Some of my drawings..." She sighed. "How am I supposed to know which ones the judges will like?"

Her mother smiled gently and blew on her tea before taking another sip.

"Choose the pieces that speak to you the loudest. The ones that show others who you are. Those are the ones that will get you into that school." Then Jen's mom left the room as quietly as she had entered it.

The sun had fully risen by the time Jen started flipping through the canvases, trying to decide which ones to include.

A grape bounced off her head and rolled under her easel.

"Hey!" Jen looked up to see her brother, John, standing in the doorway, holding a bag of grapes. He grinned at her and popped one into his mouth.

"Whatcha doing, pest?" he asked.

"How am *I* the pest in this scenario?" Jen laughed. Her brother was annoying—like all brothers were. But if she was being honest, she had to admit that he was one of her favorite people. They always had each other's backs.

John came into the room and held out the bag of grapes. She took one and looked around the room.

"Which ones do you think I should bring to my audition?" she asked, waving her arms wildly. "I can't decide! Can you help?"

John popped another grape into his mouth and threw an arm around his sister's shoulder.

"Let's take a look, little sis," he said, steering Jen toward a pile of watercolor paintings in the corner.

Chapter Two

After about fifteen minutes of wading through the various pieces scattered around the room, Jen had a nice pile of art for her audition.

"I like this one a lot," John said, holding up a watercolor that Jen had added beadwork to. It had taken ages to get the beading right, and she still had a bruise on her finger from poking it repeatedly with a needle. But the work was one of her favorites.

She seemed to prefer the ones to which she'd added what she liked to call "Indigenous flair."

"Yeah. Do you think the judges will like it too?" she asked.

"If they don't, they're idiots," he said.

"Who's an idiot?" their mother asked, walking back into the room. She stood behind Jen and smoothed her daughter's long dark hair, something that always made Jen feel calm and peaceful. And also strong.

"No one. Yet." She grinned. "John helped me pick out my audition pieces. What do you think?"

Her mother leafed through the pile.

"I love these ones." Her mother smiled, running her fingers over a couple of watercolors embellished with beads. "I'm proud of you for using traditional art in your work."

Jen beamed with pride. "But do you think the judges will like them?" she asked.

Her mother cocked an eyebrow at her and smiled.

"If they don't, they really are idiots."

John laughed loudly and handed Jen the bag of grapes as he started to leave the studio.

"Where are you going, nistes?" she asked, using the Cree word for "big brother."

"School. I have to get ready or I'm going to be late."

"You better get ready too, pîyesîs," her mother said. She always called Jen "little bird" because she flitted about from place to place. "Your dad's waiting in the kitchen."

"Crap! I didn't know it was so late! I need to have a shower," said Jen as she ran out the door. "John, wait! I need to go first!"

Chapter Three

Jen was in and out of the shower in record time. Back in the studio, she placed her artwork carefully into her portfolio.

"Are you almost ready?" her father asked from the doorway, his red hair still wet from the shower.

"Did you beat John to the shower too?" she asked.

"Of course. I jumped in while he was in the kitchen making a sandwich." He grinned at her, his blue eyes crinkling up at the corners. Just like her brother's.

"Can you carry this one?" Jen shoved a canvas almost as tall as she was at him. "And this one too."

Her dad fumbled with them at first, then lifted them up easily.

"Got 'em."

"Okay." Jen looked around the room one more time. "I think I'm ready." She picked up her portfolio, slung it over her shoulder and followed him out the door to the car.

She hadn't thought she'd be nervous. She knew she had as good a chance as anyone of getting into the school. She had worked hard and created the best artwork she was capable of creating. But her stomach was alive with butterflies, and her feet were jittery. Her father kept up a steady stream of conversation that she knew was designed to distract her.

It didn't work.

Jen smiled and tried to interject a "yeah" or "mm-hmm" at appropriate intervals, but all she could think about was the audition. All her friends would be going to the same high school, where, as far as art went, the best they could hope for was some general painting and sketching instruction. Jen had outgrown those classes a while ago. She'd never be happy there. She wanted to be in a place where she could push herself to create better art and meet new people who loved expressing themselves creatively as much as she did.

Was that too much to ask?

She sighed.

"You okay, my girl?" her dad asked, glancing at her.

"Yeah. I guess."

"Nervous?" He reached over and took her hand, which she figured must be pretty clammy and probably disgusting. He didn't seem to mind though. Jen nodded then blurted out what she had been thinking the entire car ride.

"Dad, what if I don't get in?"

She hadn't wanted to admit her greatest fear

out loud. Because saying it out loud meant it might actually happen. Saying it out loud made it a real possibility.

The car pulled into the school parking lot. Jen looked at the sign above the front door—*School of the Arts*. She wanted to belong here more than anything.

Her dad was facing her now.

"Sweetie, do you remember what I told your brother when he started dancing?"

Jen looked away from the sign and looked at him blankly. "What?"

He smiled gently. "When John started to dance, he was really worried about what other people would think. He worried he might not fit in with the other kids. Remember?"

Jen nodded. Her brother had gone through a lot in order to dance, and she had watched how he dealt with people being mean or downright racist to him.

"Do you remember what I told him?" her dad asked.

"You told him to remember who he was."

"That's right," her dad said, nodding. "And I'm going to give you the same advice now." He took her hand again. "This school would be lucky to have you, Jen. You're talented. You're creative. And you're unique." He looked at her thoughtfully. "You know, you remind me so much of your mother. And I don't just mean how you look." My brother looked like my dad, and I was the spitting image of my mom. Same dark hair and eyes, same deep-brown skin.

"Really?"

"You do. You share so much of who you are in your artwork. The school has to appreciate that. Don't let anyone tell you you don't belong here. Remember who you are."

"Okay. Thanks, Dad." She kissed him on the cheek.

"Are you ready to go in there and knock 'em dead?" he asked.

"Absolutely," she said, grabbing her portfolio and swinging out of the car.

Chapter Four

Jen walked underneath the *School of the Arts* sign and through the double doors. The halls were full of kids looking as lost as she felt. Some were carrying an instrument case of some kind. There were guitars. Flutes. Clarinets and saxophones. One kid was carrying a keyboard. There was even a kid with a tuba wrapped around himself. At the front of a long line Jen saw a sign taped to a table—*Music Department Auditions*.

Lined up at another table were kids in dance clothes. One guy was tapping nervously. Literally tapping. Like, tap dancing. Jen watched a girl in pink tights do some fancy ballet moves. Beside her another girl bent all the way over until she was basically folded in half. This was definitely not Jen's check-in table.

Then Jen spotted a line of kids holding giant portfolios and sculptures and canvases of various sizes. *That* was her table.

"Dad. Over here."

She led him over to the line and shifted from one foot to the other while they inched forward. It felt like hours before they finally reached the head of the line.

A bored-looking girl with cat-eye glasses and shockingly blue hair looked up at her. "Name?"

"Jen. Er, I mean, Jennifer. Jennifer McCaffrey."

The girl looked past Jen and frowned.

"Can I help you, sir? Are you looking for your son or daughter?"

Jen realized the girl meant her dad. *Not this again.*

"Nope. I'm good," said her dad. He smiled, putting a hand on Jen's shoulder.

"Oh," said the girl, still frowning. "Well, we need a parent or guardian to sign new students in."

"Okay." Jen's dad was still smiling. Jen wasn't. She should have been used to this by now, but each time it happened, it made her blood boil. Everybody just assumed they weren't related because they looked so different. If it bothered her dad, he never let it show. "Where should I sign?" he asked.

"Are you her...?" The girl trailed off, clearly hoping one of them would fill in the blank.

"He's my *father*," Jen said through gritted teeth.

"Oh! Okay then. Sign here, please." The girl smiled and gestured down the hall. "The art auditions are being set up in the cafeteria. It's down the hall on the left. You can't miss it." She leaned in conspiratorially. "You know, I have a friend who was adopted."

"I'm not—oh, forget it." Jen turned her back on the girl. "Come on, *Dad*."

Jen's dad grinned. "Right behind you, *daughter*."

She wished she could be more like him and not let scenes like this bug her so much.

Another girl was standing outside the cafeteria.

"I'm sorry, sir," she said to Jen's dad. "Students only from here on. But you can wait here until her assessment is done."

"Okay. Thanks."

Jen's dad pulled Jen to the side and handed her the canvases he had been carrying.

"Do you have everything?" he asked.

"I think so." Jen's voice quivered a little. She couldn't help it. She was *really* nervous now.

Her dad pulled her into a hug and kissed her head.

"Remember, there is no one like you, my girl. This school would be lucky to have you as a student. Just go in there and be yourself. Show them what you can do. You've got this."

Jen nodded. She took a deep breath and turned toward the cafeteria.

"Don't forget!" her dad yelled as she walked away.

She nodded back at him. *Remember who you are.*

She stepped into the room with her head held high.

Chapter Five

It had been three weeks since her art school audition but it felt more like three months. Jen was sure she had checked the mailbox a million times since then.

"Did the mail come yet?" John asked, perching on the arm of the living room couch.

"No," Jen grumbled. "Why is he always so late?"

"Because he's trying to drive you insane," John replied.

"Obviously."

"I was kidding, Jen."

"I wasn't! Acceptance letters were supposed to go out last week." She shrugged. "I just want to know. Know what I mean?"

"You're going to get in, Jen," John said.

"How do you know? There's no way you could know that!"

"I'm your nistes, remember? Older brothers know everything."

Jen rolled her eyes and stared out the window. "Where *is* he?"

She jumped off the couch and began to pace back and forth.

"Jen, you have to relax. There's no way you didn't get in."

Jen threw herself back down on the couch. "I just want to know for sure!"

"If they don't accept you, then it's not the kind of place you'd want to be anyway."

"If they don't accept me, I'll be stuck at the crappy public school around the corner."

"Hey!" John laughed. "*I* go to that crappy public school!"

"I know. Sorry. It's not really crappy—"

"It's just not art school," John interrupted, finishing for her. "I'm going to make a sandwich. Do you want one?"

"Are you ever not hungry?" Jen asked. "Seriously. I don't know how Mom and Dad can afford to feed you."

John was just about to answer when they heard the unmistakable *thunk* of the mailbox closing at the front of the house.

"OH MY GOD!" Jen leapt up and bolted toward the front door. John was right behind her.

"Is it here?" John asked, peering over Jen's shoulder as she pulled a big pile of mail out of the narrow metal box.

"I don't know. Give me a second." Jen flipped

through the envelopes until she reached one near the bottom of the stack. *School of the Arts* was stamped in the upper left corner.

Jen stared at it.

"Was that the mail?" Jen's mom popped her head into the room. "Did your letter come?"

Jen nodded.

"What does it say?" Her mom looked more nervous than Jen felt, if that was possible.

"I haven't opened it yet," Jen said.

"I'll open it!" John reached for the envelope, but Jen batted his hand away.

"No! I'll do it. I just need a second."

Jen's hands were shaking. She was trying to imagine what she'd do if it was bad news.

"OH MY GOD, JEN! Just open it!" John cried. He tried to grab the envelope again.

"Okay! Jeez." Jen slid a finger under the flap of the envelope and slowly swiped across.

"Oh, come on," John groaned.

"Don't rush me!" Slowly, carefully, Jen lifted the flap of the envelope and pulled out the single piece of paper, folded in thirds. She wondered briefly if one page was a good or bad sign. It wouldn't take a lot of space for them to tell her thanks but no thanks.

She held the letter for a moment without unfolding it. She glanced up at her brother, who looked like he was about to burst. Then she looked at her mom, who smiled and nodded encouragingly. Jen looked back at her hands and took a deep breath.

She unfolded the letter and scanned the first few words.

Dear Ms. McCaffrey,

We are pleased to inform you—

"Oh my god, I got in!" Jen screamed.

Before she could keep reading, John had lifted her off her feet and was twirling her around. "Way to go, little sis!"

Her mom stepped closer to hug both of them.

"We have to call Dad," Jen squeaked.

Chapter Six

The *School of the Arts* sign over the door looked more intimidating than Jen remembered. Maybe it was the font. Jen looked around to make sure no one was watching, then pinched her arm. She was really here! It wasn't a dream. She looked around nervously. Starting a new school was daunting enough. Starting one where she didn't know even a single person was enough to make her want to run straight back to the subway station, go home and hide under her covers.

On the steps there were tons of older kids calling out greetings to each other and hugging like long-lost friends. But after a few minutes Jen noticed some students who were clearly here for the first time like her. They walked alone, glancing around nervously, just like Jen was.

She recognized one girl from the auditions. Her art display had been set up right beside Jen's. She had some pretty amazing portraits that she had painted in different styles. Jen remembered one large canvas in particular. The subject had been painted in bright colors instead of skin tones. She had chatted with the girl about it briefly.

Jen jogged to catch up to her.

"Hey!" she said, falling into step beside her. "Sabrina, right?"

"Yeah, hi!" The girl looked so relieved that Jen thought for a second she was going to hug her.

"And you're...Jen! Oh my gosh, I'm so glad to see a familiar face. I was debating turning around and running home."

"So was I!" Jen laughed. "I'm glad we don't have to."

"Me too!" Sabrina linked her arm with Jen's and pulled her toward the door like they had known each other all their lives. "Clearly we're meant to be best friends."

"Oh, definitely," Jen said. She had liked Sabrina instantly, and walking into the school with a friend was a lot easier than trying to edge through the crowds on her own. "Come on. Let's get our timetables."

They found the desk where a teacher was handing out packages for all the ninth graders.

"Last name?" the teacher asked. She didn't seem very excited about being there. Jen really hoped this wasn't her new art teacher.

"McCaffrey," Jen said.

The teacher searched through a stack of oversized envelopes. "Jennifer?"

"Yes. Jen."

The teacher glanced up at her and frowned. "Pardon me?"

"I like to be called Jen," Jen explained.

Sabrina giggled. The teacher frowned at her too and then handed Jen a large envelope. "Next."

Jen stepped to the side and waited for Sabrina to get her package.

"What a charmer," said Sabrina as she joined Jen. "Thanks for waiting. Which classes do we have together?"

It turned out they had most of their classes together, except that Sabrina had Spanish while Jen had gym, and Jen's French class was at the same time as Sabrina's gym class. Their first class was art, which Jen had been hoping for.

"Looks like the art studio is that way," she said, looking at the map that was included in the package. "It's a bit of a walk. We'd better hurry or we're going to be late."

"So I was wondering something…you're Indigenous, right?" Sabrina asked as they made their way to the other end of the school.

"Yeah."

"But isn't McCaffrey a Scottish name?"

"Irish. My dad's Irish," Jen told her.

"Oh, cool. I'm kind of a mix too, but we have some Irish in there." She grinned at Jen. "Another thing we have in common!"

Thankfully, their art teacher, Miss Henry, was not at all grumpy and seemed excited to be teaching the class. Her messy, curly hair was tied back casually, and she wore paint-spattered jeans and a David Bowie T-shirt. She started by telling them how she had traveled all over the world, studying different art forms.

"She's amazing," Sabrina whispered to Jen, who was perched on a stool beside her.

"Yeah, she's super cool, all right," said Jen.

"Do you think I'd look that cool with a nose piercing?" Sabrina asked.

Jen studied her new friend's face, then nodded.

"You totally would," she whispered back.

Miss Henry explained what she wanted from her students. "So we'll definitely be working on technique, but I also want you to work on pieces that you're passionate about. Show me what you want to learn. You're all here because you're talented artists. I want us, as a class, to learn from each other."

Jen loved her already.

"So we get to work on whatever we want?" Sabrina asked.

"Yes! I want you to try new things and really stretch your artistic muscles. Your projects for grading will be things you choose to work on. You just have to run them by me first."

No art teacher Jen had ever studied with had let her do whatever she wanted. She wasn't even sure what she wanted to start with! Painting? Charcoal?

Pastels? Maybe some portraits? Definitely some beading. She opened her notebook to jot down a couple of ideas.

"And one more thing," Miss Henry continued. "At the end of term, we will be having a big art show where students can display their very best pieces." Art show? Jen looked up with interest. "Not only will your families be invited, but there will be artists, critics and dealers here as well. There will also be gallery owners and graphic design firms in attendance. They are looking for students with real potential for summer internships. So you need to work hard and make sure your projects show off your unique skills."

Jen looked at Sabrina with her mouth hanging open. An art show with the possibility of internships and who knew what else? It was too much. This day was just getting better and better. Jen was *really* glad she hadn't run home to hide under the covers!

"Okay, that's it for today, class. I want each of you to bring in your portfolio tomorrow so you can share your best work with the class. It's good to get used to having people look at your art and give feedback."

There was a buzz as students started gathering up their things and heading to their next classes.

"This is so exciting," Sabrina said. "I want to work on some really huge portraits—like the ones I had at the audition."

"Yeah, those were amazing!" Jen said.

"And...oh my god! Actual gallery owners and critics and other artists looking at our stuff? It's crazy!" Sabrina exclaimed. "What are you going to work on?"

"I'm not sure yet," said Jen. "I'd love to do something with beading on it." She shrugged. "Maybe I'll see what everyone thinks tomorrow and go from there."

All the way down the hall to English, Jen thought about her art project. The endless possibilities of what she could create. And she knew, without a shadow of a doubt, that she belonged here.

Chapter Seven

"Where is it?" Jen muttered to herself. She was looking for room 213—which *should* have come right after 212— but she turned the corner and found herself staring at room 220. "Oh, come on!"

"Are you lost?" asked someone with a deep voice.

The voice had come from behind her shoulder. Jen spun around and then looked up. Waaaaay up. Into the face of a friendly-looking boy with a shock of blond hair falling into his eyes. He shoved it out of the way.

"What? Oh. Yeah. I think so."

"Which one were you looking for?"

"Room 213. Which you'd think would come right after 212, but apparently it doesn't."

"It's around the corner on the left." He pointed in the other direction. "You went right."

"Of course I did. Why would it be left?" Jen asked.

"I have no idea. But it is."

"Are you in tenth grade?" she asked.

"No. Ninth."

"Me too!" Jen smiled. "I haven't figured out where all my classes are yet though."

The boy laughed. "Me neither. But my locker is down that hall. So I saw 213 when I walked past. And for the record, I thought it was weird too—213 should be on the right."

"I know, right?" She laughed with him. "I'm Jen."

"Dan. Daniel. Dan."

Jen looked at him, one eyebrow raised.

"Your name is Dan Danieldan?"

The boy shook his head. "No. Just Daniel. But you can call me Dan."

"Oh!" Jen laughed. "That makes more sense."

"There you are!" called Sabrina as she rounded the corner. She smiled at Dan. "Hi!"

"Sabrina, this is Dan. Dan, Sabrina. He's in ninth grade."

"Hi, Dan. Nice to meet you." She grabbed Jen. "C'mon, we're going to be late for English."

"Maybe I'll see you guys later?" Dan asked. He had a killer smile.

"Bye!" Jen called over her shoulder as Sabrina dragged her toward their class.

They ran through the door to room 213 just as the bell rang.

"Right on time, ladies," a bearded man in a Spider-Man hoodie called out. "There are two seats right up front here."

Sabrina rolled her eyes at Jen but took one of the seats. Jen glanced at the books already stacked on each desk. *The Perks of Being a Wallflower. Lord of the Flies. The Secret Path.* She looked over at Sabrina and grinned. She had already read *Perks* and loved it. And her family had gone to see a screening of *The Secret Path* film last year. And after learning absolutely nothing about Indigenous issues at her last school, she was really excited to discuss Chanie Wenjack's story with her class. It was definitely going to be a good year.

The bearded man turned and wrote his name on the board. "So, as you can see, I'm Mr. Sutherland. Do we have any readers here?" Jen and Sabrina's hands shot into the air, along with many others in the class. "Amazing! As for the rest of you, you're all getting F's." He laughed along with the class before going over the reading list and then launching into a monologue about graphic novels and comics being every bit as important as other kinds of books.

It seemed clear to Jen that unlike at her last school, the teachers were young and cool and really seemed to want to be here. They wanted to connect with the kids and get them excited about learning.

Later, as they walked out of English and headed toward the cafeteria, Jen and Sabrina kept up a steady stream of chatter about the reading list—which they both thought was awesome—and the teacher, who they both agreed was cool.

Dan fell into step beside Jen.

"Hey. Do you mind if I eat with you guys? I don't know anyone else, and you're the coolest people I've met so far."

And just like that, on her very first day, Jen had two new friends.

Chapter Eight

"How was your day?" Jen's mother asked, setting a platter heaped high with pasta and dripping in her dad's famous sauce down in the center of the table.

"Dad cooked?" Jen asked, breathing in the familiar scent of tomatoes and oregano.

"I did indeed," her father said as he stepped into the dining room. He was carrying a tray of garlic bread, hot and fresh from the oven.

Jen scooped a few heaping spoonfuls of pasta onto her plate and grabbed a slice of garlic bread.

"So? How was it?" her dad asked.

"It was really good!" Jen said. She bit into the garlic bread, and butter dripped down her chin. Her mother handed her a napkin. "Thanks."

"And your classes?" asked her mom.

"Good so far. Math looks like it's going to be hard. But the reading list for English looks pretty cool. We're reading *The Secret Path*! And my art teacher is letting us create whatever we want for our assignments."

"That's amazing," Jen's mom said. "Have you made any new friends?"

"Yeah, two. Sabrina, who's in a few of my classes, and Dan, who's new too."

"Are they as dorky as you are?" asked John and then winked at her.

"Yes. Yes, they are," Jen said, sticking out her tongue at him.

"So tell us about them," her dad prompted.

"Well, I met Sabrina at the audition. She paints portraits mostly. Really big ones. She's amazing." Jen took another bite. "And I haven't seen any of Dan's artwork yet, so I'm not sure what he does. But he's really nice." She shrugged.

"A boy?" Jen's dad raised an eyebrow at her.

Jen rolled her eyes. "Yes, Dad. He's a boy. Girls can be friends with boys, you know."

"Of course they can," her mother said and touched her hand. "And your new friends sound very nice."

"They are," Jen said, smiling at her.

"Except for being dorks," John said.

"You're just jealous," said Jen. "Anyway, we're supposed to bring our portfolios to art class tomorrow, so I have to update mine and make sure all my best stuff is there."

"What will you bring?" her mother asked.

Jen chewed thoughtfully on her piece of garlic bread.

"I'm not sure yet. Some beading. Some of my multimedia pieces. I want to try more of that in class. And some sketches. Can you guys help me look through my stuff again?"

"You bet," her brother said.

Her mom and dad nodded.

Jen smiled at them. She was lucky, she thought. Her family really was one in a million. No matter what happened, she could always count on them to support her.

Chapter Nine

"I'm so excited!" Sabrina said, almost bouncing up and down in her seat. "I can't wait to see everyone else's portfolio. Aren't you excited?"

"Yeah." Jen slid into the seat beside her friend and put her portfolio on top of her desk. "Hey! There's Dan. Dan! Over here!" She waved at her friend. "I didn't think you were in this class."

"Yeah, you weren't here yesterday, were you?" Sabrina chimed in as Dan took the seat beside Jen.

"I was in the office. They messed up my schedule, and they had to fix it before I could come to this class." He shrugged before heaving his portfolio onto the desk.

"Good morning!" said Miss Henry, rushing into the room just as the bell rang. She was holding a steaming cup of something out in front of her so she wouldn't spill it. Despite her caution, a little splashed out onto the floor. "Oops. Let me just grab a paper towel before someone slips on that." The scent of coffee hit Jen, who was close enough that the liquid had splattered her desk a bit. "Sorry about that. Jen, right?" Miss Henry wiped up Jen's desk and then the floor. "Jen, since I almost scalded you, why don't you get us started with your portfolio?"

"Okay." Jen nodded and moved to the front of the class. She opened her portfolio wide. The first piece was a watercolor painting of the apple tree in her backyard. Resting on one of the branches was a beaded blue jay.

"Whoa," Dan said. "That is so cool!"

"You did this beading yourself, Jen?" asked Miss Henry.

She nodded. "Yeah. My mom taught me how to bead when I was a kid. I just took it up again last year because I wanted to try to incorporate traditional art into my modern pieces."

Miss Henry nodded approvingly. "That's great, Jen. Thank you for sharing." She briefly talked to the class about how effectively the beadwork worked with the watercolors. Jen saw a few kids at the back rolling their eyes and whispering to each other. She ignored them. Dan and Sabrina were grinning at her, and she smiled back before turning the page and showing another beaded piece. Then another. The fourth piece was something different. It was a black-and-white photo she had taken of herself, using a timer. She had torn the photo in half and replaced the missing part with a color sketch of her face. It was supposed to represent feeling invisible and colorless sometimes and feeling strong and full of life at other times. She thought she had done a pretty good job.

The kids in the back were whispering to each other and giggling again. Jen ignored them. Her next piece was a charcoal sketch of her brother in full regalia, dancing at a powwow. A kid at the back raised his hand.

"Yes?" Jen asked, happy that her classmates seemed interested.

"So do you only do, like, Indian stuff?" The other kids in his little squad tittered.

"*Indian* stuff?" she repeated coolly before Miss Henry could interject. "If you mean do I focus my energy on creating Indigenous art that reflects who I am as a person and an artist, then yes. I guess I do." Jen smiled at Miss Henry, closed her portfolio and walked back toward her seat.

Sabrina held out her hand for a high five. "Great job," she said before turning to shoot a dirty look at the kids in the back.

"Yeah, that was amazing," Dan agreed. "Ignore them."

Miss Henry reminded everyone that they were here to share and support each other as Dan took his portfolio up front. He showed a bunch of full-color pages from various comic books he had created. He had spreads of superheroes and villains fighting epic battles and even a page where the hero and the girl share a passionate kiss. That one got him a bunch of hoots and whistles from the kids at the back. He quickly closed his portfolio and sat back down.

"Wow," said Jen, looking at him intensely. "You're really talented."

"Yeah? Thanks," he said, blushing. "I read a lot of comics. Obviously."

Soon it was Sabrina's turn. Her smaller portraits were no less amazing than her giant ones. She had done ones in charcoal and oil paints, pastels and sketched out with pencil. Some were incredibly realistic, and some were more impressionistic or fantastical.

Jen and Dan congratulated her as she sat down.

"Amazing!" Dan told her.

"Seriously. Your portraits should be hanging in a gallery somewhere," Jen agreed.

Sabrina grinned. "Well, with any luck..."

The rest of the presentations were impressive too. The students were all really talented. Of course, Jen had known they would be, or they would never have gotten into the school. And they were all so different! It was pretty inspiring to see the distinctive styles and abilities. Jen realized there was a lot she could learn, not just from her teacher, but from her classmates as well. As she stood up at the end of the class, she thought about how lucky she was to be there.

Then she heard the whispers behind her. It took a moment for her to realize they were talking about her.

"She probably got in purely as a minority applicant," someone was saying. "It's really not fair that she took a spot from someone who deserved it more."

"The school probably gets government funding for having her," another kid said. "You know, like how they get to go to university for free and don't pay taxes? Why else would she be here?"

Jen's face burned as she spun around.

"I got in the same way you did," she said, stepping toward the group until she was almost nose to nose with one of them—the same boy who had asked if she "only did Indian stuff."

"Hey!" Sabrina stepped up beside Jen. "What did you say to her?"

"Jordan didn't say anything to her!" one of the girls in the group said.

Dan was beside Jen and Sabrina in an instant. "He said something *about* her though."

"I just think people should get in based on talent and not as a token minority," said Jordan, shrugging.

"Did you *see* her artwork?" Sabrina demanded. "Jen is more talented than any of you."

"Yeah, she may be in a minority, but that's not why she's here, and you know it. You're…you're just jealous!" Dan spat out.

"Guys, forget it," said Jen. "It's fine. Let's just go. People like them aren't going to change their minds." She grabbed her friends' arms and pulled them away from the group.

"God, they're idiots!" Sabrina fumed as they walked down the hall.

"Yeah, well, I'm used to it," said Jen.

Chapter Ten

John was already at home, telling their mother about an exercise he'd done in drama class, when Jen got back from school. Her mother was laughing with him but looked up when Jen walked in.

"Oh hi, sweetheart. How was your day?" her mom asked.

"Fine," Jen said without stopping. She walked straight past the kitchen and toward her bedroom.

"Do you want something to eat?" her mom called out.

"No, thanks." Jen closed the door to her room so she wouldn't have to answer any more questions. She dropped her backpack on the floor and fell onto her bed.

She shouldn't have been surprised that there were kids at her new school who thought it was all right to judge her based solely on the color of her skin. It wasn't anything new to her. But it still hurt. Especially when she had thought things would be different at an art school. Somehow, she had convinced herself that the kids would be more tolerant of each other.

Jen rolled onto her side. A picture of the whole family in a frame John had made for her for her birthday a few years back sat on the night table. With a pang of guilt, Jen stared it and wondered, not for the first time, if things would be easier for her if she looked more like John. More like her father.

And less like her mother.

Chapter Eleven

It was easy enough for Jen to avoid the most racist kids at school. She wasn't their only target anyway. Anyone who didn't look exactly like they did got the same kind of treatment. The questions about whether they belonged there or if they were there only because they filled some kind of imaginary minority quota. The whispered accusations that they had taken the place of someone who deserved it more.

She could stay out of their way mostly.

And even when she couldn't, she had Dan and Sabrina beside her, friends who had her back.

"Did you understand the math homework?" Sabrina asked over lunch, pushing her math book across the table. "It went completely over my head."

"Me too. I was going to ask Dan for help," Jen said with a grin. "Sorry."

"Do you think there's the slightest chance I'll use algebra again after I graduate? Like, ever?" Sabrina asked, staring at her math book like it was written in a foreign language.

"Probably not, since you'll be a famous artist traveling the world and painting portraits of royalty."

"Nah. I'm going to paint portraits of regular people doing regular things in their regular places. I want to show average people. Not just the super rich."

Wow. Jen stared at her friend. Sabrina was 100 percent certain about her ambitions. But Jen hadn't quite figured out what she wanted to do with her life.

She knew she wanted to be an artist. But exactly what form that would take or where it would take her…well, she wasn't quite sure yet. The fact that Sabrina had it all figured out already was cool…but a bit depressing at the same time.

Dan slid into the seat across from Jen.

"What are we talking about?" he asked, stuffing a fry into his mouth.

"Algebra," Sabrina said and moaned.

"Hey, Dan, do you know what you're going to do after high school?" Jen asked.

"Sure. I'm going to get a job with Marvel and create a new comic-book series starring diverse superheroes."

Holy crap! That plan was just as good as Sabrina's! Jen felt even more deflated.

"What are you doing to do?" Dan asked Jen.

"Umm…I'm not sure," she stammered. "I haven't… umm…I haven't figured it out yet." Her friends had their lives all planned out, and she hadn't even thought about what she'd be doing in a few years!

"Well, you're only fourteen," Sabrina pointed out, stealing one of Dan's fries.

"You're both fourteen too!" Jen cried. "And you have it figured out already. I don't even know if I want to travel or where I want to work or if I want to get an art degree..." She trailed off. "My big goal was to get into this school. I didn't think past that."

Dan pushed his fries toward Sabrina.

"Isn't that what this school is for though?" he asked. "We get to try so many different things here. We get to figure out who we are as artists."

Sabrina nodded. "And we can figure out what we want to do along the way," she said. "You never know. I might change my mind and decide to open up my own gallery in Paris."

"And I might do—nah, forget it. I'm working for Marvel," Dan said.

"I guess you're right," Jen said. "But I still feel like I'm behind everyone else."

"I guarantee you, half the kids here have no idea what they want to do after graduation," Sabrina told her.

"You think?" Jen asked.

"Probably more," Dan agreed. "Give it time. And if you don't figure it out, you can be my assistant."

Jen laughed. "I'll keep that in mind. And not to change the subject or anything, but did you get what we were supposed to do for algebra homework? Because Sabrina and I are both lost."

Dan pulled his book out of his bag and started explaining everything, slowly and patiently. Jen picked it up pretty quickly, so while Sabrina caught up she looked around the cafeteria. She was trying to decide which students had their lives figured out and which ones, like her, still felt like little kids.

Chapter Twelve

Jen was working on her first art project of the year. It was a charcoal sketch of an Indigenous woman wearing a beaded medallion. She had done a couple of rough versions, but the woman kept coming out looking like her mom. Jen didn't want that. So she'd set the charcoal aside for the time being and brought her beading supplies to class. While the other kids worked with paints, pastels, colored pencils and clay,

Jen picked up tiny beads on a needle and sewed them onto a piece of felt. She used a second needle to stitch them into place.

"That looks hard," Sabrina said, looking over from the giant canvas she was working on. From what Jen could see, it was a picture of a child jumping in a puddle, wearing flowered rain boots.

"It was at first. But I've been doing it for years. Now it's kind of relaxing." She glanced at Sabrina's canvas. "That's looking good."

"Thanks! It's my sister."

"I didn't know you had a sister," Jen said.

"Yeah. She's five. Loves to dance."

Jen smiled. "My brother's a dancer too."

"Oh yeah?" Sabrina frowned at her canvas, then shaded a spot in the puddle. "Is he younger than you?"

"No. Older."

"Really? What kind of dance does he do? Hip-hop?"

"Hip-hop?" Jen giggled. It was hard to picture John doing hip-hop. "No, men's Fancy Dance mostly."

Sabrina looked up from her picture. "Men's fancy... what?"

"Oh, sorry! That's a kind of traditional dancing. He's really good, actually."

"That's cool. I've never seen that kind of dancing. My sister just does ballet and tap."

"Yeah, he competes and everything."

"Wow." Sabrina nodded. "Do you do fancy dancing too?"

"Me? No. I don't dance at all."

"Me neither."

Dan joined the conversation.

"I took dance," he announced. "Five years."

"You did?" Jen asked.

"Let me guess. Jazz!" Sabrina said. "No, wait. Tap! I can totally see you tap-dancing."

"Nope." Dan shook his head. "Ballet."

"You took ballet? Wow," Jen said.

"Yeah. My mom took me to see *Billy Elliot*, and that was it. I decided I wanted to be a dancer."

"So what happened?" Sabrina had forgotten her canvas and was studying Dan with great interest.

Dan shrugged.

"I don't know. I got into creating my own comics. Then I got the chance to take some classes with an artist from Marvel Comics. But they were at the same time as my ballet class. That's when I realized I loved drawing more than I loved dance. I just wanted to make comics."

Jen was struck again by how her friends really knew what they wanted to do with their lives. And that she most definitely didn't.

"Oh my god," a voice stage-whispered from a few desks away. "Can't she do *anything* else?"

"I know, right? I mean, we get it. You're Indian."

Jen felt the heat rise up her neck until she was pretty sure her cheeks were blazing. Sabrina started to stand up, but Jen put a hand on her arm.

"Leave it," she muttered.

"They can't get away with talking like that!" Sabrina said.

"It doesn't matter, Sabrina. I'm—"

"But—" Dan interrupted.

"No," Jen said firmly. "It doesn't matter. I don't care what they think." She made a point of not looking at the kids who were whispering. "Just leave it alone."

She stared at the medallion she was working on and turned it over in her hands. She glanced over at the kids watching her and whispering together. Then she turned back to her beading. With a sigh, she stuffed the medallion into the box of beads and needles and scissors, and closed the lid with a snap.

Chapter Thirteen

The whispered words of that group of kids stayed with Jen for the rest of art class and through every other class she had that day. She thought about them on the bus ride home and on the short walk from the bus stop to her house.

Can't she do anything else?...We get it. You're Indian.

She shook her head, trying to loosen the words and get rid of them once and for all. But they wouldn't budge.

She *was* an Indigenous artist! That's who she was. But for some reason that made her stand out. And not in a good way. She knew she hadn't been accepted into the art school as some token minority. She had earned her spot. But hearing the accusation over and over, day in and day out, made Jen question herself. She was starting to wonder if she really belonged there.

She stood at the kitchen sink and looked out the window to the backyard. Her dad was standing at the barbecue, wearing an apron that said, *World's Best Dad*. Jen and John had given it to him the past Father's Day. He wore it every single time he grilled. Tonight he was flipping burgers and singing along to a tune blaring out of the portable radio he had placed near the barbecue. From inside the house, Jen couldn't tell what it was. Probably some classic rock. Or David Bowie. Or maybe it was Drake. For some reason, her dad loved Drake.

Jen's mom was in her garden, picking tomatoes. The vines were heavy with the huge, ripe vegetables. Or were they considered fruit? Jen could never remember.

She studied her mom. She was so opposite to Jen's father. Dark where he was light. Quiet where he was loud. Thoughtful where he was impulsive. She could see that her mother was saying something to her dad and laughing, but Jen couldn't hear what it was. Watching her dad smile back and wave his spatula at her made Jen smile too. She loved how easy her parents were with each other.

John was bouncing on the trampoline, doing flips. First front flips. Then back. He was really good. Jen had taught him some of her gymnastic moves because he wanted to do flips like some of the other dancers. Learning on the trampoline was the easiest way to master them—there was less chance of breaking a limb. Like their dad, John had an easy smile and a contagious laugh. And he was good at everything. The kind of guy everyone liked. He seemed to drift between things pretty effortlessly. He danced and played soccer and had friends in both groups. He got good grades, and girls loved him. Everything came easy to him. Everything.

Jen shook her head. She closed her eyes, trying to shake off the negative feelings that had come over her. She wished she could have it as easy as her brother did. She *wanted* to be Indigenous. She was *proud* to be Indigenous. But she couldn't help but think how much easier it would be if she looked more like her brother.

Chapter Fourteen

Jen spent the next morning—Saturday—getting ready for a powwow her brother would be dancing at. She cleaned her lenses and repacked her camera bag. She'd be taking pictures only of John and the other dancers she knew. Some dancers didn't like having their regalia photographed, and Jen respected that.

She had chosen to wear the ribbon skirt her mother had made for her. It was red and black with stripes of ribbon sewn around the bottom half. She paired it with a pair of moccasins and a black T-shirt that had *Warrior* across the front in red letters. It was one of her favorite outfits. She braided her hair and headed down to the kitchen with her camera bag.

"Hey! Are you almost ready?" John asked. He liked to eat before he danced, so he was surrounded by a variety of mostly empty plates. He finished a corner of toast and gulped down some orange juice.

"How you manage not to throw all that up, I will never understand," Jen said mildly. "Seriously. It's disgusting how much you eat."

"Hey, it takes a lot of energy to be as awesome as I am," John said. "Are you going to eat anything?"

"I'll take a banana," Jen said. "Where are Mom and Dad?"

"Working. I'm driving."

"Well then, let's go." Jen picked the keys off the counter and threw them to him. "We have to get going or we'll miss the Grand Entry."

The ride to the fairground was far from quiet. John was blaring A Tribe Called Red on his car stereo while keeping up a steady stream of conversation about the dance he had been working on. He was pretty excited.

"It's going to blow your mind," John said as they pulled into the parking lot. "Make sure you get a good seat."

"I will. Good luck!" she called as he ran off to get ready.

Jen found a spot close enough for her to take some decent pictures and settled in, standing for the Grand Entry and even joining in a Circle Dance.

"I love your shirt," a woman told her as Jen sat down to wait for John's dance.

"Thanks a lot," Jen said. She loved going to powwows. No one ever looked at her funny or questioned if she belonged. She *did* belong.

When Jen heard her brother's name being announced, she got her camera ready, making sure her telephoto lens didn't have any dust on it.

As soon as John started dancing, Jen zoomed in, getting a truly great photo of him. He looked fierce. He was concentrating on the drumbeat and dancing his heart out. Jen kept clicking, half-standing to get another shot and then crouching down for a slightly different angle.

John was brilliant. His new routine was even more exciting than his last one. As she watched him twirl one way and then another, she even forgot to take photos for a minute. It felt like every single person was holding their breath.

But then Jen heard people talking behind her.

"That's awful," someone said. "Why was he even allowed to dance?"

Jen felt her heart drop all the way into her stomach.

"He must have lied about his background when he signed up."

"He should be kicked out," someone else said.

Jen felt like she was going to throw up. But then she saw the smile on John's face when he executed a perfect backflip. He kept smiling as he held his last position as the drumbeats faded. She stood up and turned around, her face burning.

"That's my brother down there, and he has as much right to be here as you do," she said. Without waiting for a response she left to find John.

She found him talking to his friend Sam, who was congratulating him on his performance.

"You've really stepped up your game, man," Sam was saying. "You looked amazing out there!"

"Yeah, well, I learned from the best," John replied.

Sam was his teacher, and Jen knew he had been one of the biggest influences on her brother.

Jen nodded at Sam. "Aren't you dancing, Sam?" she asked.

Sam was wearing jeans and a T-shirt that said, *Not Today, Colonizer*. It made Jen grin. He gave her a one-armed hug.

"Hey, cousin," said Sam. "No. I hurt my shoulder,

so I'm out for a bit while it heals. But this guy did me proud." He slapped John on the back again.

"Did you get some good pictures?" John asked.

"I did! But I'll show you once I've had a chance to edit them." Jen was itching to leave. "Meet you by the car?" she asked. The powwow had been ruined for her, thanks to those horrible people in the audience.

"Oh," said John. Jen could see that he was surprised, but she didn't care. "Just give me a few minutes, okay?" he added, handing her the keys.

Jen took the keys and headed out to the car. She wanted to think about whether she should tell her brother what had happened.

Chapter Fifteen

"So what did you think of my new routine?" John asked, pulling away from the parking lot and heading back toward home.

Jen shifted uncomfortably in her seat. She had decided to tell him what had happened, but she wasn't sure where to start.

"It was really good. I got some great pictures, I think."

"Awesome." John was drumming his fingers on the steering wheel. "And...?"

"And it was fun."

"Really? Because you sure wanted to get out of there fast. I thought maybe you hadn't had much fun. Or maybe there's something else going on?"

Jen sighed.

"Yeah, well, there were some people sitting behind me..."

"Okay," said John.

"And...and they were saying stuff."

"Right."

"About you."

"Ah." John smiled at her. "So what was it they were saying?" he asked gently.

"They said...they said you didn't belong there. That you shouldn't have been allowed to dance. That you must have lied when you signed up." Jen wiped at her eyes angrily.

"And that made you mad?" John asked.

"Yes! Of course it did! You worked so hard to learn to dance. You have as much right to be there as anyone. And I told them that," Jen said.

"But you know I belong there. And I know. So why does it matter what anyone else thinks?" he asked.

"It...it just does!" Jen exclaimed. "I mean, why should they be allowed to say things like that?"

John shrugged. "People can say whatever they want, Jen. I don't look Cree like you and Mom, so people question me. It happens all the time. It happened at my dance class too, remember?"

"Yeah. But that doesn't make it right."

"No," John agreed. "But it's always going to be this way for me. Whenever I go to a powwow, there will always be someone questioning whether I belong there."

"I thought it must be easier for you," Jen admitted. "Being light-skinned."

"And I always thought it would be easier to be dark-skinned like you!" John grinned.

"There are kids at my school who say I only got in because I'm a 'minority artist.'" Jen said the last bit with air quotes.

John shrugged.

"You *are* a minority artist. A really good one. And of course you didn't get into the school based on the color of your skin! You got in because you're super talented. And now you have a great opportunity to share your vision. You have a voice. Use it."

"You sound just like Mom and Dad." Jen smiled at him.

"Yeah, well...they're pretty smart."

They drove in silence for a few minutes. But then Jen spoke again. "The thing is, at my school, I just don't feel like I belong," she admitted.

John nodded and then did a quick U-turn.

"Let's go someplace where we both belong," he said.

Chapter Sixteen

"Where are we going?" Jen asked, punching John in the arm.

"You'll see! We'll be there in five minutes—calm down."

"You know I hate surprises," Jen reminded him.

"That's because you have zero patience."

"So? I still hate surprises."

"You'll like this one," John promised. "Look. We're already here."

He had pulled the car into the parking lot of the community center where Jen used to take art classes.

She looked at him, puzzled. "What are we doing here?"

"Come with me and you'll see." John jumped out of the car. Jen was right behind him.

The first thing they heard when they walked through the front doors was the faint sound of drums echoing down the hallway.

Jen looked at her brother, who was smiling widely down at her.

"Well, come on," he said.

They followed the sound of the drums until they were standing outside the gym doors. John pulled them open and stepped inside. As Jen followed, she heard at least twenty girls screaming as they threw themselves at her brother. "John! It's John!"

Jen took a step back. Actually, she was kind of shoved out of the way, because her brother was being mobbed by his former dance mates. Jen hovered at the edges of the love fest. She found herself standing beside a woman she recognized as John's first dance teacher.

"Hi," she said shyly. She had only met Santee a few times and was a little intimidated by the beautiful woman who was so graceful and much more comfortable with herself than Jen was.

"Jen!" Santee enveloped her in a hug. "It's so nice to see you again!"

"You too." Jen hugged her back.

Santee looked at the girls surrounding John.

"Girls, let him breathe!" she exclaimed, laughing. "What brings you back, John?" she asked, pulling him away and hugging him hard. "What are you doing here?"

"I thought Jen could use a dance class," he said.

"Wait—what? I can't dance!" Jen blurted out.

"Sure you can," John told her. "Taylor! Can you teach my sister how to dance?"

A girl that Jen recognized, not just from the community center but also from the powwows, stepped forward.

"If I can teach you how to dance, I can teach anyone," she told him. She grabbed Jen's hand and pulled her into the middle of the floor.

John laughed. "Hey! I turned out pretty well!"

Santee walked over to her phone and started scrolling. Jen realized that was where the drumbeats were coming from!

"Why don't you prove it?" Santee said to John, shoving him toward a group of girls. "Jen, you stick with Taylor. She'll show you what to do, okay?"

As the music soared through the gym, Jen looked around at the other girls. They had already started moving and swaying to the drumbeats. Jen seriously considered bolting for the door.

"Don't even think about it," Taylor said. "Your brother had that same look on his face the first time he came in here. Don't worry. Just watch what I do, and you'll get the hang of it pretty quick." As she talked, Taylor was doing a little tapping step that seemed pretty straightforward. Jen copied her.

Santee walked around the room, keeping an eye on all the dancers. "That looks great, Jen! Hey, John, check out your sister's footwork," she called. "She's a natural."

"Yeah, unlike him," Taylor whispered, and Jen laughed.

"I heard that!" John made his way over and watched Jen move through the routine with Taylor. "Looking good, sis. Just listen to the drums. As long as you hear the drums, the steps will follow." Then he danced away again.

"You've got it!" Taylor said. "Want to try a turn now?"

Jen nodded. She was afraid to talk in case it threw her off. Taylor demonstrated a turn beside her, then spun back the opposite way.

Jen gave it a try. She kind of made it.

She glanced up, saw John dancing with a group of girls and smiled. He looked at home here. And hearing the drumbeats and the sound of laughter as the girls danced, Jen realized she felt at home too.

"Let me try that again," she told Taylor, spinning first one way, then the other. She heard the drums and didn't falter for a second.

Chapter Seventeen

After her dance lesson and her talk with John, Jen felt more confident going into art class on Monday. She belonged here, she told herself. She even said hi to the kids who had been hassling her. They looked shocked by her friendliness, which made her feel great. She was not going to sink to their level. She smiled at Dan and Sabrina as she took her place beside them.

The big art show was only two days away. Jen was on track to have her beaded piece finished and ready to go the day before. That was when all the students' artwork had to be set up. She had finished most of the painting, and although the figure at the center still looked a little like her mother, she was pretty happy with it. The woman in the painting was proud and strong, staring out of the canvas as if daring anyone to challenge her. Jen had modified the simple beaded medallion she had started with into a unique beaded necklace of intertwined roses of different sizes. It was by far the most intricate thing she had ever beaded, and she still needed a couple of hours to finish it. She had this class, lunchtime and after school. If it wasn't finished by then, she was out of luck.

While her friends concentrated on their pieces for the show, Jen threaded her needles and got to work on the necklace, making sure it was just the right size for the neck of the woman in the painting.

She picked up six seed beads with one needle and stitched them down with a second needle. She had to be careful not to rush, so that her beads would all line up perfectly and lie flat.

"That looks amazing, Jen!" Dan leaned over from his desk and studied her beadwork. "Is it really hard to do?"

"No. Not hard exactly. I mean, it was at first. I stabbed myself a *lot*. But I've been doing it for so long now that it's kind of relaxing."

"I don't know how you can even see well enough to get those tiny little beads on the needle," Sabrina said, looking over Jen's shoulder.

"My mom has to wear reading glasses when she beads now." Jen smiled and picked up another bunch of beads. The edging was almost finished. Maybe fifteen more minutes and she could attach it to the portrait. She was so looking forward to the art show. And she was actually more excited than nervous, which was kind of a surprise. The idea that someone could offer her an internship, or a critic might like what she had done, was more than she could wrap her head around. So she was trying not to think too much about it and focus on just getting her work finished.

In fifteen minutes—okay, it was actually closer to thirty—she was done. And the necklace was spectacular. Jen was pretty impressed with herself. She'd never made anything this intricate before.

"Whoa! Could you make one just like that for me?" Sabrina asked.

"Where would you wear it?" Dan asked.

"Prom! Picture day! Babysitting. Seriously, I could wear that anywhere."

"Well, maybe. We'll see," Jen said. Then she carefully, very carefully, attached the necklace to the painting and stepped back to admire her work.

She was finished. And really happy with it. It was as perfect as it was ever going to be.

Sabrina slung an arm over her shoulder and squeezed it hard.

"That is *amazing*, Jen. Man, this art show is going to be awesome. Hey, come and take a look at mine."

After checking out Sabrina's and Dan's projects, which were super impressive too, Jen started cleaning up the table and putting away her beads. She was so absorbed in her chatter with Sabrina and Dan and with getting her supplies organized that she didn't even notice the group of kids whispering and staring at her back.

Chapter Eighteen

By the end of the day, all anyone could talk about was the art show. With students feverishly trying to finish up the last bits of their work, no one was paying any attention in class. When the final bell rang, Jen automatically fished in her bag for her phone. It wasn't in the pocket she usually kept it in. She stuck her hand into the larger pocket. It wasn't there either. She went through the pockets of her bag one by one, pulling things out and piling them on the floor at her feet. Her phone wasn't in her bag.

"Damn," she muttered, shoving everything back into her bag.

"What's wrong?" Dan was leaning against the wall beside her, studying his own phone.

"I lost my phone," she said.

"Well, where did you see it last?" he asked, sounding way too much like Jen's mother.

"I don't know. Wait. I took a picture of my project with it. I must have left it in the art studio."

Dan followed her down the hall, toward the studio. They passed Sabrina at her locker on the way, and she fell into step beside them. Their conversation was about the art show. All their projects were done, so they had an easy night ahead.

Jen stepped into the studio. She knew exactly where she had left her phone and hoped it was still there. Tracking down her teacher to get it back would be a real pain. She stepped toward the easel where she had left her beaded portrait. She felt something crunch under her foot. She looked down and then stopped so suddenly that Dan and Sabrina ran into her.

"What are you—?" Sabrina broke off. "Oh no."

"What?" Dan hadn't seen it yet. But the second he did, his face clouded with anger.

The floor was covered in beads. Jen reached out a shaking hand and turned the easel toward her. The necklace had been destroyed. Only a few random beads clung to the canvas. The portrait itself had been slashed from corner to corner.

"It's ruined," Jen whispered, reaching out to touch the tattered edges.

"Well...maybe we can fix it," Sabrina said desperately. She dropped to the floor and started scooping up beads. "Dan, help me!"

"Just leave them, Sabrina. I can't fix this," Jen said dully. "It took me days to do the beading alone. It's too late."

"We should go to the office," Dan said.

"Why? What good will that do?" Jen asked.

"We need to report what those idiots did!" Sabrina said.

"We can't prove it was them," Jen replied.

"Of course it was them!"

"I know that!" Jen spun around to face her friend. "But what does it matter now? It'll be their word against ours. My project is already ruined."

Dan touched her shoulder.

"What do you want to do, Jen?" he asked.

"I can't deal with this right now. I just want to go home." Jen turned her back on her easel and the ruined mess of her art project. She walked out of the studio without looking back.

Chapter Nineteen

There was a place Jen always went to think things through.

The trampoline in the backyard.

There was just a feeling she got when she was jumping—when she was almost flying—that made things a little easier to bear.

So she jumped.

And waited for that feeling to hit her. The feeling that everything was going to be okay. Because right now *nothing* was okay. Her painting was ruined, and there was no way she could fix it. Even if she could have redone the portrait, the necklace was completely destroyed, beads lying all over the studio floor. It would take her days to recreate that necklace.

And the art show was tomorrow.

The kids who had been telling her she didn't belong since the day she'd started at the School of the Arts had made sure she couldn't prove them wrong.

So she jumped. She jumped and tried to clear her mind.

"I could teach you how to do a backflip on that, you know," a voice called out from across the yard.

"How long have you been there?" she asked her brother. She followed her question with a perfect backflip just like the ones she had taught *him* to do.

John shrugged.

"Show-off," he said, pulling open the netting and climbing onto the trampoline with Jen. They both jumped without saying a word for a minute or two. But then John broke the silence.

"So...what's going on, little sis? You're jumping like you've got something on your mind."

Jen didn't answer. She just kept jumping.

"Uh-oh. That bad?" John asked. "Is there anything I can do?"

Jen stopped jumping.

"No. I don't think so." Her eyes started to well up with tears.

"Hey, are you okay?" John stopped and put his hand on Jen's shoulder.

Jen thought for a second and then nodded. "Yeah, I'm okay, thanks. I just need to think."

"All right." John gave her a quick hug, resting his chin on the top of her head for a second. "I'll leave you to it."

The second her brother was off the trampoline, Jen started jumping again. She didn't know what she was going to do about her art project yet, but she could jump.

Chapter Twenty

This time, though, not even bouncing on the trampoline could help. Completely bounced out, Jen did a final backflip, climbed down and closed the netting behind her. She grabbed her sneakers and padded to the house in her socks. It drove her mother crazy when she did that.

Jen stopped at the sliding doors into the kitchen, spotting her family through the glass. She stood in the fading light and watched them, trying to see what other people saw when they looked at them.

Her mother was standing at the stove, stirring whatever she was making for dinner. Probably chili. She was smiling at John, who was standing behind her. He tried to dip a spoon into the pot to sneak a taste. She smacked his hand away playfully. Jen watched as John wrapped an arm around his mom. His skin pale against hers. His red hair standing out dramatically from her dark braid. Jen knew that the effect was exactly the same when she stood beside her brother. Or when she stood beside her father, who was setting the table, his thick red hair standing up like he had been running his hands through it.

People looked at John and thought his skin was too light to dance at a powwow. People looked at Jen and thought her skin was too dark, that there was no way she would have gotten into the School of the Arts based solely on talent. She was too Indigenous for people, and John wasn't Indigenous enough.

And when people saw them together, they inevitably tried to figure out who belonged and who didn't. Who was related and who wasn't.

Jen watched as her parents laughed together at something John said. Her father walked over and kissed her mother on the cheek, then messed up John's hair. Now they looked even more alike.

To Jen they just looked like her family. But to other people, they looked like they didn't fit together.

Still carrying her shoes, Jen walked around the house and entered through the side door. She didn't want to talk to anyone right now. Without turning on the hall light, Jen tiptoed down the hall to her studio. She sat down at her easel and stared out the window. Thinking about her family. Thinking about the art show. Thinking about what other people saw when they looked at her and John and what she saw when she looked at him and at her parents. Then she picked up a pencil and started sketching.

Chapter Twenty-One

Jen worked through dinner. Her mom brought her a bowl of chili and a plate of buttered toast.

"Are you okay?" she asked. Jen dipped a piece of toast in the bowl and chewed absentmindedly, studying the drawing in front of her. She tore the page off and crumpled it up, throwing it in the garbage with the dozens of others she had discarded.

"Mm hmm," she nodded, starting a new sketch.

"Is there anything you need?" her mom asked.

"No," she said, erasing a line and filling it back in again. Her mother slipped out of the room. Jen kept drawing. Later, her father came in to collect her dishes.

"What are you working on?" he asked.

"I don't know. Just trying out something new," she told him, not looking up.

"Well, we're watching a movie if you want to join us."

"Nah. But thanks. I want to keep working on this."

Jen continued to work. She could hear her family laughing in the TV room. It got darker and darker outside. She barely looked up when her parents leaned in the doorway of the studio to say good night.

"Can we see what you're working on?" her dad asked, taking a step toward Jen.

"Not yet. Let me see if it's going anywhere first," she said.

"Don't stay up too late, pîyesîs," her mother said as she and Jen's dad turned to go.

Jen waved a brush in their general direction.

She had switched from charcoal to paints now. She had never quite got the hang of oil paints, so she was working with acrylics. The house was quiet and dark around her, but Jen kept painting.

She vaguely noticed the grandfather clock in the front hall chiming one o'clock. John stuck his head in the doorway.

"You okay?" he asked.

Jen grunted in response.

"Do you want to tell me what's going on?"

Jen glanced over at him, then tossed her brush into a container of water and turned away from her painting for the first time in hours. Her shoulders were sore, and she rolled her neck from side to side, feeling it pop.

"Someone completely destroyed my art project today. The art show is tomorrow—oh, I guess that would be tonight now—and I have nothing to display."

"Wait, someone *destroyed* your project? Who? Why?"

"It doesn't matter. I have my suspicions, but I can't exactly prove it. And anyway, I can't let them win, you know? This art show is an amazing opportunity for me, and I can't let a couple of jerks keep me out of it because they don't think I belong."

"What has been going on at that school?" John's freckled face was red with anger.

"It doesn't matter! I *do* belong there. And I'm going to prove it. But I only have a few hours left to create something as good as the piece they trashed."

"What can I do?" John asked.

"Just let me work," Jen told him, turning back to her canvas and grabbing a new brush.

She wasn't sure how much time had passed, but after a while John came back long enough to put a steaming cup of tea down beside her.

"I figured you could use this," he told her, squeezing her shoulder before retreating.

"Thanks," Jen muttered, reaching down without looking and taking a long sip of tea. Then she added a slash of blue to the canvas.

Chapter Twenty-Two

Jen didn't sleep.

At all.

She did close her eyes for about twenty minutes early in the morning, after being absolutely, 100 percent positive that she had set the alarm on her phone. The second it went off, her eyes snapped open. Her paintbrush was still in her hand.

Around eight thirty her brother popped into the studio. "Do you need a ride to school?" he asked.

"No. I'm not going."

"Did you tell Mom?"

"No," Jen muttered.

"Well, I'm going to."

John disappeared. Jen kept painting.

A few minutes later her mom came in, her face a mask of concern.

"What's going on, Jen? John told me your artwork got destroyed!"

"He told you?"

"Of course he told me!" She pulled her phone out of her pocket. "I'm calling the school."

"No! Mom, I'm handling it. I need to figure this out myself."

"They need to do something about this!" said her mom. Jen had never seen her this upset before.

"Mom, *I'm* doing something about it. I'm not going

to let anyone force me out of the show. I need to prove I belong there."

"To who?" her mom asked.

"Myself. And I can't do that if you call the school and get the art show cancelled or something."

Her mom studied her face, then sighed. "Okay. But the school needs to know what happened."

"I'll tell them after the show. Just let me stay home and finish this. I'll talk to my teacher after. I swear." Her mom was caving. She could see it. "Mom, please call the school and let them know I'm staying home. Go to work. I'll be fine."

"All right. But we're dealing with the school later."

"I know. And you and Dad will be on time?"

"Of course." Jen's mom kissed her head and disappeared out the door.

Jen didn't have a minute to spare, but she pulled her phone out and texted Dan and Sabrina.

Staying home to work on something. See you tonight.

She turned her phone off before they could respond. She wasn't even sure she had enough time to finish but she had to try. Jen stared at the painting, dabbed on another bit of red, then took it off the easel and propped it against the wall to dry. She grabbed another canvas—a blank one—and put it on the easel. She pulled a pencil from behind her ear and started sketching. Her mom appeared again briefly, to drop off a muffin and a glass of juice.

"Here, you need to eat something. But we're going to talk later. John will drive you to the art show and your dad and I will meet you there. Okay?"

"Uh-huh." Jen heard but didn't see her mom go. She wasn't hungry. She wasn't even tired really. She was just focused. Focused on finishing the project that was burning a hole in her brain and focused on proving once and for all that she belonged.

As the day wore on, Jen moved between canvases, touching one up, adding something to another. She mixed paint with a medium to give it texture. She used one color here and another there. Dabbed on one canvas and used a broad stroke on another. Hours that felt like days passed until finally, after less than twenty-four hours, Jen was finished. She lined up her three canvases and studied them. They were as good as they could be.

Jen glanced at the clock. She had just one hour to change and get over to the school to set up.

"John!" she bellowed. "We need to leave!"

Chapter Twenty-Three

"Do you want me to come in with you?" John asked. "If those kids start messing with you, I'll have your back."

"I'll be okay. Thanks for the ride. Just go find Mom and Dad. You can see everything once I have it all set up." Jen pulled the canvases out of the car. She had covered them with soft tarps. She didn't want anyone to see them until they were ready and up on easels. She wrestled them carefully through the front door and down the hall to the studio.

Literally every pair of eyes turned when she walked in. Jen had been dreading that.

But she'd have to worry about it later, because right now all she had time to do was get set up before the critics and gallery owners and guests arrived.

"Jen!" She had barely had time to prop her canvases against the wall before she was wrapped in a gigantic hug from Sabrina and Dan. "We have been trying to call you all day!"

"Yeah. Sorry. I turned my phone off. I had too much to do."

"Did you fix your painting?" Dan asked.

"How did you get your beading done so quickly?" Sabrina interjected.

"I didn't. I made something new."

They stared at her and then in one smooth movement stepped in front of her. Jen saw the group of kids who had been harassing her since the first day of school walking toward them. Two were missing, Jen noticed. A boy and a girl whose names she had never bothered to learn.

"Don't even think of doing anything," Sabrina warned them. "Jen hasn't said anything yet about what you losers did, but I will."

"Me too!" Dan spat out.

"We just came over to say that we're sorry. Jordan and Sydney were the ones who wrecked your painting," one of the girls said.

"We had nothing to do with it," added one of the boys.

His name was Nick, Jen knew.

"Yeah, right." Sabrina took a step toward him.

"I'm serious. We had no idea they were going to do that. They were laughing about it. It wasn't right." He shook his head.

"We went to Miss Henry and told her. They got suspended."

"What?" Jen squeaked. She had not been expecting that.

"We really are sorry. Your painting was amazing," the girl said.

"Yeah," Nick agreed. "It really was."

"Thanks." Jen nodded, relieved that she could focus on the art show and not worry about what she was going to do about the vandals. It had been taken care of before she could get involved. And an apology from kids who had followed the other two? It was more than she would have imagined. "Listen, I have to go and get set up."

The kids walked back to their own artwork. Jen turned toward her friends.

"Can you find two more easels for me?" she asked Dan. As he ran off, Jen said to Sabrina, "Well, here goes nothing."

"Jen?" Miss Henry touched her arm. "I'm so sorry about what happened. I called your mother earlier...

and I tried to call you. I want you to know that we don't tolerate bullying at this school. I think we need to sit down and talk about what happened." She smiled kindly. "It's great that you came to support your friends after what happened."

"Oh, I'm not just here to support them. I'm showing my own work too."

"But your piece...?" Miss Henry frowned.

"Was destroyed. Yes. But I think I have something even better to show tonight." She gestured at the canvases. Miss Henry smiled.

"Then I better let you get to it. I can't wait to see what you brought, Jen."

Jen's heart was racing. She couldn't wait for everyone to see her new artwork either.

Chapter Twenty-Four

"Well?" she asked, standing with Dan and Sabrina in front of the three easels. "What do you think?"

"Wow," Dan said. "It's really powerful."

"Is that how you feel?" Sabrina asked.

"Yeah. That's how people see me and my brother," she said, gesturing to the paintings to the left and right of the one in the center, "and that's how I see us."

She pointed to the middle canvas, which was twice the size of the others.

It was a painting of her family. Her father stood proud and strong, holding a traditional Irish walking stick called a shillelagh. His mother, Jen's nana, had brought it with her from Ireland. Jen had managed to make her dad's blue eyes sparkle like they did in real life, and his red hair was a burnished-copper color. Jen had painted her mother beside him, her hair tightly braided the way she wore it most days. She was holding an eagle feather her father had given her when she was a child. John stood beside their mother in his dance regalia. He looked exactly like their father, and Jen had tried to capture the expression he always got when he danced at powwows. John was proud to be part of both worlds and, in ways Jen hadn't begun to understand, felt comfortable in both. In the painting, Jen stood beside her father. Looking so much like her mother and leaning on her father just like she did every day of her life. The portrait showed a strong, proud family who loved and supported each other through everything. The painting had turned out just the way Jen had hoped.

On the canvas to the right was a painting of John in a T-shirt that showed his pale Irish skin. He held a paintbrush to his arm, coloring his white skin a deep brown.

The canvas to the left showed Jen in a matching T-shirt, holding a paintbrush to her brown arm and painting a long streak of white on it.

Others might see her family and decide they didn't belong together, that their skin was the wrong color, but the painting in the middle showed who they really were. Jen's chest swelled with pride as she heard whispers of appreciation around her. Her classmates were watching, and for once she didn't care what they thought.

"That's amazing," one of the kids said, patting her on the back.

"Well done, Jen," said Miss Henry. "I am very impressed."

"Thanks," she said, smiling. She looked at the clock. She was ready for whatever was going to happen tonight.

Chapter Twenty-Five

People were arriving in a steady stream now. Three of the first visitors to come through the studio door had been Jen's family. Now they stood together in front of the display, in exactly the same order that Jen had painted them.

"Oh, Jennifer," her mother said, her eyes wet with tears. "It's beautiful."

Her father sniffed loudly.

"Dad, you're not crying, are you?" Jen asked.

"No! Well, maybe." He hugged her tightly. "I'm really proud of you, my girl," he said, kissing the top of Jen's head.

"Me too, little sis," John said. "And am I really that badass? Because I look pretty badass."

"Nah. I took pity on you," Jen said.

"Hey!"

"I'm kidding! You're a total badass."

She introduced her family to Sabrina and Dan, and then they all went over to admire their artwork.

"Your friends are really talented," John said.

"Of course they are," said Jen. "They got into the School of the Arts, didn't they?" She winked at John.

She didn't have much time to talk after that. Despite the fact that she hadn't slept, Jen was buzzing with excitement. No one asked if she was adopted. No one asked if John was her foster brother. They just looked at her artwork and told her how powerful it was. They gave her business cards and shook her hand. They congratulated her and asked questions about which mediums she liked to work in and where she saw herself after high school. It was all incredibly thrilling.

Things worked out the way they were supposed to, Jen realized. Her original piece had been beautiful, and she had put a ton of work into it. But she had put her heart and soul into this one.

"Hi," said a smooth voice behind her. "Are you the artist?"

"Yes." Jen turned, holding out her hand. "I'm Jen McCaffrey." Then she gulped. "Holy cow! You're Anna Bessette!"

The woman smiled. "I am."

Anna Freakin' Bessette was standing right in front of her! She was a painter who created portraits that were full of life and that told stories of the people in them. Jen adored her.

"I'm a huge fan of your work!" she gushed. "I went to see your latest exhibit twice!"

"Thank you so much. What can you tell me about this piece?" she asked.

She was talking to Jen like she was a real artist. Jen beamed and took a deep breath to shift out of fan-girl mode before she answered.

"Well...the painting in the middle is my family. My dad is Irish, and my mom is Cree. This is how I see them. Proud and strong. Supporting each other. A normal family whose members are proud of where they come from."

Anna nodded.

"This one is my brother, painting his skin brown to fit with what some people believe he should look like. The other is me, struggling to belong."

"So what other people see as opposed to what you see?" Anna asked.

"Exactly!" Jen said.

"It's pretty amazing," Anna said.

Jen thought she might pass out. Anna Bessette thought her paintings were amazing!

"Not just the execution, which is exceptional," Anna continued, "but the whole concept." She smiled at Jen. "I'd love to see more of your work."

"Are you serious? I have my sketchbook here. I could show you that."

She spent ten minutes showing Anna Bessette some of her sketches and then the photos she had taken with her phone of the beaded necklace before it was destroyed. Anna studied the photo and then handed back the phone.

"You're really talented, Jen. Listen, I have an exhibition coming up, and I could use an assistant to help me get organized. It wouldn't interfere with your schoolwork at all. Mostly weekends. Would you be interested? It's a really great way to get to know the business side of the art world."

"Would I...yes! Oh my god, I'd love to!" Jen looked at her mom to make sure it was okay. Her mom nodded with a huge smile on her face.

"Great!" Anna handed Jen a card. "Call me in a day or two, when you've recovered from this, and we'll set up a time for you to come by."

"I will. Thank you so much!" She shook Anna's hand and watched as she walked away.

Sabrina jumped on Jen the second Anna was gone. "Oh my god!" she said. "Anna Bessette wants you to be her assistant? That's amazing!"

"I know. I can't believe it," Jen said, still in shock.

"I can," Sabrina told her, giving her a hug.

"Me too," Dan said, grinning widely.

"Me too!" her entire family added at exactly the same time.

Jen laughed. In the middle of the studio, surrounded by all the people she cared about, Jen was right where she belonged.

Acknowledgments

A huge thanks to the Orca pod—especially Andrew and Tanya. I am thankful beyond words for your belief in me. And to my agent, Amy, who puts up with endless emails from me and who is the greatest champion any writer could hope for. Thank you as well to the student who painted the picture that inspired this story. I don't know who you are or even remember which school I was visiting. But I saw your painting hanging in the hall and it has stayed with me ever since. The idea of a person painting themselves another color to be accepted is a painful and powerful one. I hope, wherever you are, that you know that your art touched someone and inspired them deeply.

Read on for an excerpt from

HE WHO DREAMS

The sound of drumbeats
changes everything.

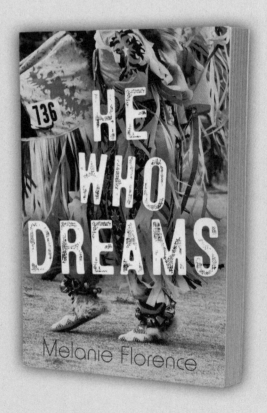

Soccer star John surprises everyone when
he signs up for Indigenous dance classes.

Excerpt

"Okay, ladies, facing forward. This is John, and he's going to watch what you do and follow along. It's his first class, and he's just another student today, so let's go easy on him, okay? So everyone say hi and then forget he's here."

"Hi, John!" The girls giggled and stared at me.

Santee turned to me. "So traditionally, you'd learn to dance by following the older dancers and doing what they do. But since you're the oldest person here, you'll follow the more experienced dancers." She waved a hand around the room while the girls laughed and poked each other.

"Hi." I waved, my cheeks burning. They were all staring, so I tried to think of what made my sister laugh and did a low, theatrical bow to the class. They collapsed against each other in fits of giggles.

"Okay then," Santee said. "Facing forward. You too, Taylor. So, John, just try to follow along. We'll keep it simple and take it slow."

I nodded, shifting my weight nervously from foot to foot.

"Great. Okay...music! And let's start with a simple step and step and—knees higher, John. Good! Feel the music, class. I want to see everyone floating." Santee stepped in front of me. "It's a little different for men. Instead of that single step they're doing, you want to do kind of a double step. Don't put your heel down, but land on the ball of your foot. So lower your heel, but don't let it touch. No, don't let it touch. You're letting it touch."

"Okay, okay." I looked up at her, then back down.

"Stop looking at your feet! Chin up. Shoulders back. You should be dancing with your whole body even when you're just doing simple steps. And stay light on your feet. This is how we'd dance in a Grand Entry at powwow." She looked at me, probably trying to gauge how much I knew about powwows, before continuing. "John, at a powwow the area we dance in is called the arbor. It's sacred. The arbor is a special place where all of your good thoughts come back to you. If you dance unselfishly—for someone other than yourself, for someone who can't dance or who is suffering—if you can do that, you will truly feel the music and dance better than you've ever danced before."

I nodded and tried to remember not to put my heels down. She turned away as the music sped up. I fixed my eyes on the girls dancing in a line ahead of me and did my best to mimic what they were doing.

I watched intently, but their feet were moving so fast! And, as it turned out, I had absolutely no coordination at all. I tried stepping as lightly as the girls, but the fact that my steps were echoing off the walls was a little off-putting. And I kept forgetting to add the second tap of my foot that the girls didn't have. I thought I was starting to get the hang of it when Santee changed it up on me.

"And let's spin! Same steps, John, but we're going to add a simple spin...now!"

I looked up, panicking, and spun to the left as everyone else twirled right. I tried to correct myself at the last second, and my feet somehow got tangled together, sending me crashing to the gymnasium floor. I heard the girls laughing around me, but I couldn't bring myself to look. A small hand reached down in front of my burning face. I glanced up at the tiny girl standing over me, her glossy hair in braids and a crooked grin on her face. She smiled bigger, still holding out her hand.

As humiliated as I was, I couldn't help but laugh. She reminded me of my sister.

As I reached out and took her hand, she leaned down and whispered in my ear. "Don't worry. I fell down in my first class too."

"Really?" I asked, smiling.

"Yep." She stood with me as I rose to my feet. "Just watch me," she said. "I'll show you what to do."

The rest of the class had continued without us, so I brushed myself off and nodded at her. "Okay. Ready. Wait! What's your name?"

"Taylor. Okay. So bounce…just bounce."

I bounced on the balls of my feet. This was easy! Once I got the hang of that, I nodded at my mini teacher to continue.

"Good! Now step…you want to almost skip. But it's not a skip." She giggled at her description. "So bounce and bring your foot up and then step." I followed her. "That's great! Now try it in time to the drums."

I had completely forgotten to listen to the drums. I had forgotten everything except watching my little friend as she slowly started to turn.

"Whoa...okay. Hang on a sec." I took a deep breath and followed. I did it!

"Good job!" I heard Santee call out. I beamed and kept dancing.

"Go, John!" Taylor clapped. I spun harder. The whole class was clapping now. I was feeling pretty cocky at this point and kept spinning. Kept stepping. Kept lifting my knees. Kept listening to the drumbeats.

"Stop!" I vaguely heard someone call out, but it barely registered. I was on a roll. I was dancing! I was doing great...until I hit a cart full of basketballs and went down hard, hitting my shin and my hip on the way down.

The class ran over, hovering and cooing over me like miniature mother hens.

"Are you okay?" Taylor asked.

I rubbed my leg, grinning despite the pain. "I'm good. Did you see that? I was doing it!" I couldn't stop smiling.

Santee grabbed my hand and hauled me up. "Well done, John. It's a good start."

Taylor reached over and high-fived me. "Just wait until next week," she told me. "We'll try adding a jump."

* * *

After an hour of me stumbling my way through a series of steps and trying my best to keep up with the whirling dervishes that were the little girls spinning around me, I felt like my head was spinning around with them. They giggled their way out the door at the end of the class as I gathered up my things and tried to ignore the growing aches and pains in my body.

"You did well today, John." Santee was collecting her own things and getting ready to leave. "Did you enjoy it?"

"I did," I admitted, stretching my back and feeling a twinge of pain. It was going to hurt a lot later.

"I'm glad," Santee said, heading for the door.

"It's just..." I called out to her back, then watched her turn and look at me quizzically.

"It's just what?" she asked.

"Well, I think I'd like to come back, but I was wondering if there was a class for boys."

"Ah." Santee nodded. "I guess it must feel a bit awkward being in a class of little girls."

"Kind of, yeah."

"But unless you can drive into the city, mine is the only class around here," she explained. "I'm sorry."

"Okay. That's all right. I just wondered," I said.

She turned back toward the door. "See you next week," I called after her.

I couldn't see how I could get to the city to take a dance class. I supposed I could ask to borrow the car. But then I'd have to explain why, and I felt like

I had to see if this was something I really wanted to do before I told my parents. I had run through a long list of hobbies and sports, only to grow bored as soon as my parents had shelled out for equipment and supplies. Art classes, drama, football, hockey, a short-lived interest in scuba diving...it was a long list. Other than soccer, nothing had stuck for me.

No. I was going to pay for these lessons out of my own money and see where the adventure took me before I told my family.

Star Spider

HEY JUDE

Penny is busy enough with school and taking care of her sister. She doesn't have time for love, but then she meets Jack

Could Kipp's lucky break of landing a job and a place to live be too good to be true?

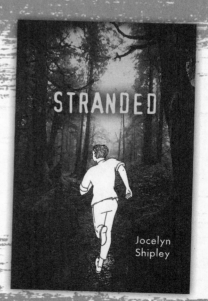

STRANDED

Jocelyn Shipley